LITTLE SIMON

An imprint of Simon & Schuster Children's Publishing Division
1230 Avenue of the Americas, New York, New York 10020

Copyright © 1996 by Oyster Books Ltd.
Illustrations copyright © 1996 by Katy Rhodes
Text adapted by Tim and Jenny Wood
Consultant: Reverend Iain Craig
Designed by Katy Rhodes

Manufactured in China
1 3 5 7 9 10 8 6 4 2
ISBN 0-689-81030-X

THE CHRISTMAS STORY

Illustrated by Katy Rhodes
Adapted by Tim and Jenny Wood

Little Simon

A long time ago, in the town of Nazareth in northern Israel, there lived a young girl called Mary. She was engaged to be married to Joseph, a carpenter. One day, God sent an angel, Gabriel, to visit Mary.

"I have some wonderful news," smiled Gabriel. "God has blessed you. Soon you will have a little baby boy."

"But how can that be?" asked Mary, puzzled. "Joseph and I are not married yet."

"God has arranged everything," explained Gabriel. "Your son will be born through God's power. Many people will call him the Son of God."

When Joseph heard that Mary was going to have a baby, he was surprised and upset. He thought that Mary might have fallen in love with someone else. But that night, as Joseph slept, God visited him in a dream.

"Don't be upset," said God. "Mary's baby is my own son. I have chosen you and Mary to be his parents. Call him Jesus and raise him as if he were your own child."

When Joseph woke, he felt as if a great weight had been lifted from his shoulders. Soon afterward Mary and Joseph were married.

In those days, Israel was part of the Roman Empire. One day, news came that the Roman Emperor, Augustus, wanted to find out how many people lived in the Empire so that he would know how much money he could collect in taxes. Everyone was ordered to go to the place where they had been born, to be counted by Roman officers.

"I was born in Bethlehem," Joseph told Mary. "I'll have to go there. You'll need to come with me."

This worried Mary. Bethlehem was far away.

"It will be hard for me to make such a long journey," she said. "The baby is due very soon."

"Don't worry," replied Joseph, hugging her. "We'll put you on a donkey, and we'll go slowly and carefully."

A few days later, Mary and Joseph set off. They stopped and rested whenever Mary felt tired. The journey took almost a week, but finally they reached Bethlehem.

"You'll soon be able to have a good rest," said Joseph.

But he had forgotten one important thing. Lots of other people had come to Bethlehem to be counted, and all the inns were full. Wherever Joseph went, he got the same reply.

"Sorry! All our rooms are taken."

Tears began to trickle down Mary's face.

Joseph tried one more door. "Do you have a room?" he asked the innkeeper's wife.

"I'm sorry—" she began.

"We're desperate," Joseph interrupted. "Our baby is due any minute."

The innkeeper's wife looked at Mary's tear-stained face. She saw Joseph's worried expression, and she took pity on them.

"I don't have any rooms left," she replied, "but I could let you sleep in the stable. It's a bit rough, but it is warm. And I can give you plenty of clean straw."

"Thank you," smiled Mary. "I am sure we'll be very comfortable."

That night, while everyone else was asleep, Mary gave birth to the baby Jesus. Joseph wrapped him in strips of cloth to keep him warm. Then he filled a manger with clean straw.

"This will make a fine crib," he announced. Mary and Joseph knelt beside the manger and thanked God for his goodness to them.

That same night, on a hillside behind Bethlehem, some shepherds were guarding their sheep. As they huddled around their campfire trying to keep warm, a bright light appeared in the sky. The shepherds looked up in amazement. It was the angel Gabriel.

"Don't be frightened," called Gabriel. "Something amazing has just happened. A baby has been born tonight in Bethlehem. He is called Jesus. One day he will save the world. You can find him in a stable, lying in a manger."

Suddenly, the sky blazed with light. "Glory to God," sang hundreds of angels. "Peace on Earth."

Then, just as suddenly as they had appeared, the angels vanished. The shepherds stared at one another.

"A baby come to save the world?" they muttered. "Let's go and see for ourselves."

The shepherds hurried down the
hillside into Bethlehem. It didn't take them
long to find Mary, Joseph, and Jesus.

"So it's true, then," they said, peering into the stable.
"There really is a baby."

The shepherds gathered around the manger. They knelt
down and thanked God for sending this little baby to save
the world. They told Mary and Joseph about Gabriel and all
the angels. Then, seeing that Mary was very tired, they
tiptoed out and went back to their sheep.

Long before Jesus was born, in a faraway place, three wise men had learned that something amazing was going to happen. They had spotted a bright new star and had looked in their ancient books.

"It is a sign that a new king will soon be born," they agreed. "We must follow the star and see for ourselves."

So the three wise men set out across the desert on a long and dangerous journey. They traveled by night so they could follow the star, and rested during the day.

After many weeks they reached the city of Jerusalem, a few miles north of Bethlehem.

"The best place to find a new king would be in the royal palace," they decided.

The wise men went to the palace and asked to see King Herod. Herod knew nothing about a baby but he was very worried by the news.

"A new king might take away my throne," Herod thought. "This could be dangerous."

But he pretended to be pleased, and sent for his advisers.

"Do the scriptures tell you where a new king would be born?" he asked.

"Yes, your majesty," replied the advisers. "In Bethlehem."

"So it is true," thought Herod. "There *is* a new king. I must find him and get rid of him. I'll trick these three wise men into finding him for me."

"You must go to Bethlehem," Herod smiled at the wise men. "Then come back here and tell me where the new king is. I must go and see him, too."

The wise men left the palace. They had no idea that Herod's smile was not sincere.

Soon the three wise men were on the road to Bethlehem. As they neared the town they grew more and more excited. They could see the star they had followed shining over a house! The house was the one where Mary, Joseph, and the baby Jesus were now staying. As soon as the wise men saw the baby in Mary's arms, they knew immediately that their long search was over. One by one, they knelt down.

"This is him," gasped the first wise man.

"The new king," whispered the second.

"We have seen him with our own eyes," murmured the third.

Then the wise men presented the special gifts they had brought. One gave a chest of gold. The second gave sweet-smelling frankincense. The third gave a fragrant spice called myrrh.

In a dream that night, God warned the wise men that Herod wanted to harm Jesus.

"Stay away from Jerusalem," God told them. "Go home silently by a different route."

Herod waited for several days for the wise men to return to his palace. Eventually he realized that he had been tricked. In a towering rage, Herod made a terrible plan to get rid of the new king. He called the Captain of the Guard.

"Go to Bethlehem," Herod ordered. "Kill every boy child under two years of age."

The captain turned pale. He had never heard such a terrible order. But he did not dare disobey Herod. Soon, Herod heard the sound of marching feet as the soldiers set off for Bethlehem.

But God had warned Mary and Joseph in a dream about Herod's terrible plan. God had told them to take Jesus to Egypt and to hide there until it was safe to return. So when the soldiers reached Bethlehem, Mary, Joseph, and Jesus were already far away and safe from harm.

And so every Christmas, we celebrate the miracle of baby Jesus' birth.